Where's My Hockey Sweater?

by
Gilles Tibo

illustrations by
Bruno St-Aubin

Scholastic Canada Ltd.

New York Toronto London Auckland Sydney
Mexico City New Delhi Hong Kong Buenos Aires

Library and Archives Canada Cataloguing in Publication
Tibo, Gilles, 1951-
[Grouille-toi, Nicolas! English]
Where's my hockey sweater? / Gilles Tibo ; illustrations
by Bruno St-Aubin.
Translation of: Grouille-toi, Nicolas!
ISBN 0-439-95677-3
1. St-Aubin, Bruno 11. Title. 111. Title: Grouille-toi, Nicolas! English.
PS8589.126G7613 2005   jC843'.54   C2005-901149-1

ISBN-13 978-0-439-95677-2

Translation by Petra Johannson.
Text copyright © 2004 by Gilles Tibo.
Illustrations copyright © 2004 by Bruno St-Aubin.
English text copyright © 2005 by Scholastic Canada Ltd.
All rights reserved.

13 12 11   Printed in Canada   119   11 12 13

MIX
Paper from
responsible sources
FSC   FSC® C103113
www.fsc.org

To Zachary

> — *G.T.*

To Jean-Félix

> — *B. St-A.*

It was Saturday. Nicholas snuggled happily
under the covers, dreaming of the day ahead.
This morning was the first hockey practice
of the season.

UH OH! Suddenly he remembered. He had to find his equipment. Quick as a flash, he jumped out of bed, tripped over his stuff, and fell flat on his face.

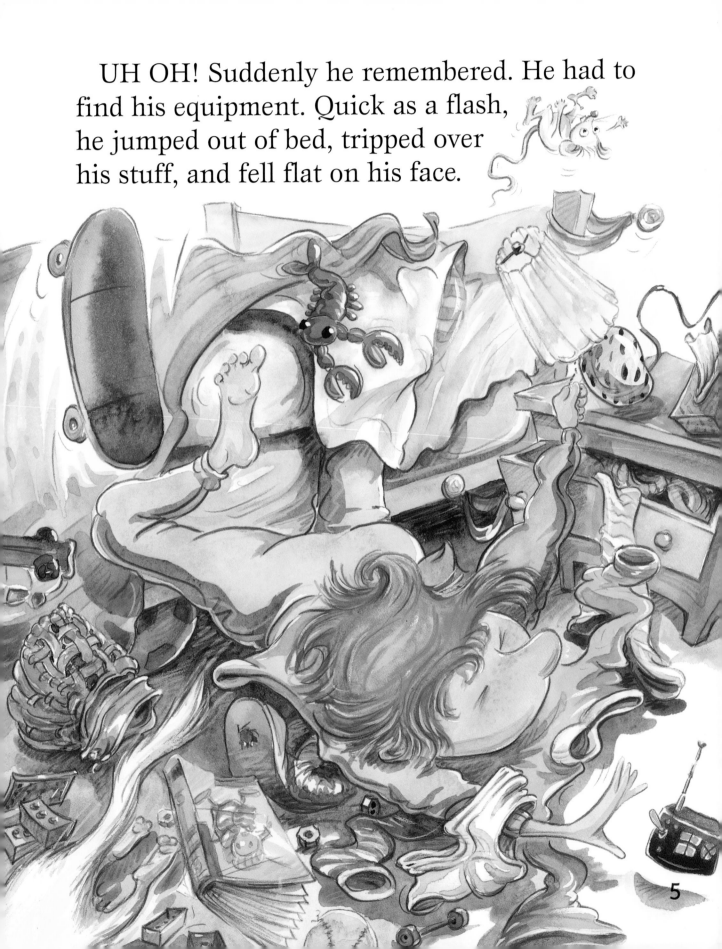

Where was his championship hockey sweater? Nicholas started searching. All he could find were shirts and socks and pyjamas. YAY! There were his shoulder pads.

Then he looked for his helmet. He found
a tuque, a baseball cap and a wizard's hat.
YAY! There were his shin guards.

Still no hockey sweater. No helmet either. And where were his skates? Nicholas found rain boots and ski boots and flip-flops. YAY! There were his hockey pants.

He hunted all over his bedroom, but he just couldn't find the rest of his equipment.

Nicholas crawled out over his mess.

His mom and dad were in the kitchen.

"You're only half dressed!" said his dad. "Hockey practice starts in an hour!"

"But I can't find my sweater or my helmet or my skates."

"I think I saw your skates in the garage," said his mom. "You've got to keep track of your stuff."

Nicholas headed for the garage. He checked the cupboards and the shelves. He searched through all the boxes. Finally, he found his skates.

Nicholas rushed back to the kitchen and gulped down some cereal. He still had to find his sweater and his helmet. And his hockey stick!

"I think I saw your helmet in the basement," said his dad. "You've got to keep track of your stuff."

Nicholas raced down to the basement. He rummaged under the workbench and behind the suitcases and through the toy boxes. Finally, he found his helmet.

Nicholas ran back to the kitchen and gobbled some toast with peanut butter. Now to find his hockey stick and his sweater.

"I think I saw your hockey stick under the porch," said his sister. "You've got to keep track of your stuff, Nicholas."

There was no time to lose. He ran outside and looked under the porch. He found pails and shovels and dump trucks, and finally, his hockey stick!

Nicholas hurried back to the kitchen and grabbed a blueberry muffin. Now he just needed to find his sweater.

"Didn't I see your sweater in your bedroom?"
his mom asked. "You know, Nicholas, you've got
to keep track of your stuff."
Nicholas ran back to his room. What a MESS!
He would never be able to find his sweater in there.

Quickly he set to work, piling things in the drawers and wedging them into the wardrobe.

Then, at the very back of the closet,
Nicholas found his hockey socks. And,
best of all, his championship sweater!

He pulled them on as fast as he could and looked in the mirror. "I'm ready to go!" he called.

His parents hurried to his room.

"Congratulations!" cried his mom.
"You look like a real pro," said his dad.
Nicholas looked at the clock. "We have to go!
The practice starts in 15 minutes!"

"Wait a second," said his mom.
"I'm not sure where I put my car keys…"